THE ONE AND ONLY
DELGADO CHEESE

Text copyright © 1993 Bob Hartman
Illustrations copyright © 1993 Donna Kae Nelson

Designed by Melanie Lawson

Published by
Lion Publishing
1705 Hubbard Avenue, Batavia, IL 60510 USA
ISBN 0 7459 2405 0

Lion Publishing plc
Sandy Lane West, Oxford, England
ISBN 0 7459 2405 0

Albatross Books Pty Ltd
PO Box 320, Sutherland, NSW 2232, Australia
ISBN 0 7324 0650 1

First edition 1993

Library of Congress Cataloging-in-Publication Data

Hartman, Bob. 1955–
    The one and only Delgado Cheese : a tale of talent, fame, and
friendship / Bob Hartman : illustrations by Donna Kae Nelson. — 1st ed.
        p. cm.
    "A Lion picture book."
    Summary: With the help of his great-uncle, a former preacher and
vaudeville star, a young boy gains enough confidence to perform in the
school talent show.
    ISBN 0 7459 2405 0
    [1. Great-uncles—Fiction. 2. Self-confidence—Fiction. 3. Christian
life—Fiction.] I. Nelson, Donna Kae. ill. II. Title.
PZ7.H267250n 1993
[E]—dc20   92-29059

A catalogue record for this book is available from the British Library.

Printed in USA

THE ONE AND ONLY
DELGADO CHEESE

● ● ●

Bob Hartman

Illustrated by Donna Kae Nelson

A LION PICTURE STORY
Oxford · Batavia · Sydney

Harvey Merritt was not the kind of boy people noticed.

Harvey was not bright enough for people to say, "Oh, what a clever child!"

Harvey was not good enough at football or baseball for people to say, "Oh, what an athletic child!"

Harvey was not especially tall, nor extremely short. He wasn't ugly. He wasn't cute. He was just plain normal. And he didn't like it.

So when he moved from the Warren G. Harding School to Edward Everett Horton Elementary School, Harvey decided to do something about it.

One Monday morning when Harvey walked into his new school, he saw a sign hanging on the bulletin board.

"TALENT SHOW:" the sign said, "SIGN UP NEXT FRIDAY AFTERNOON."

Now, as you may have guessed, Harvey Merritt was not particularly talented either. But his desire to be noticed was so great, he was determined to find *something* he could do.

Harvey's first step was to talk with his Great Uncle Kaz.

Great Uncle Kaz was the reason Harvey's family had moved in the first place. He had to stay in a wheelchair and needed someone to look after him and his big house. Someone who could cook and clean. And someone who didn't mind the occasional bursts of what Uncle Kaz called his "preachytelling" (and what his relatives called his "funny ways").

Great Uncle Kaz stayed by himself most of the time in his faded, musty bedroom at the back of the house, thumbing through his Bible and preachytelling his stories to the wallpaper birds—or to Harvey, who often wandered in for a game of checkers and ended up listening to "How the Lions Lost Their Lunch" or "The Whale's Sour Snack."

As far as Harvey was concerned, those old Bible stories of Daniel and Jonah had never been so interesting. He liked Great Uncle Kaz. In fact, of all the people Harvey knew, he felt most noticed by Great Uncle Kaz.

Uncle Kaz listened patiently to Harvey, nodding his bald, wrinkled head from time to time as Harvey talked about the school talent show poster.

"A talent show, eh? Well, what can you do, Harvey? Can you sing?"

Harvey shook his head, "No."

"Can you dance?"

"No."

"Do you know any good jokes?"

Harvey didn't.

Great Uncle Kaz thought for a moment. Then he got a look in his eye like a preachytelling was coming on.

"Harvey," he said, "do you see that old trunk beside the bed? Take the blankets off the top, open it, and bring me the first thing you find inside."

The first thing Harvey found was a paper tube with a rubber band around the middle. Uncle Kaz slid off the rubber band and unrolled the paper. It was a poster.

In the middle of the poster, which was now yellow, but was probably once white, big letters read:

"FROM THE STAGES OF ZANZIBAR, MADRID, AND GAY PAREE—DANCIN' DAN THE VAUDEVILLE MAN!"

"Who's that?" Harvey asked.

Uncle Kaz smiled a sly smile. "That was me years ago."

Harvey looked puzzled. "But Mom said you were some kind of preacher."

The old man chuckled. "The Good Lord gave me a talent, Harvey—a gift for telling stories, for getting folks to sit up and pay attention. But before the Lord grabbed hold of me to do that for him, I was Dancin' Dan the Vaudeville Man."

"What's Vaudeville?" asked Harvey.

"Oh, it's a bit like your talent show, really. A lot of people doing a little bit of everything. Singing, dancing, juggling. Acrobatics, comedy, magic acts. We weren't the best, but we enjoyed ourselves. That was the most important thing—for me anyway."

Uncle Kaz stopped. Like a light bulb had switched on in his head.

"Harvey," he said, "the Good Lord gave us all talents. Not all of us the same ones. Not all of us the same number. But he didn't pass anybody by. And the road to finding those talents starts with what brings us joy. Harvey, what do you enjoy?"

Harvey's light bulb lit as well. Sure, there was something he enjoyed doing. He liked to do…

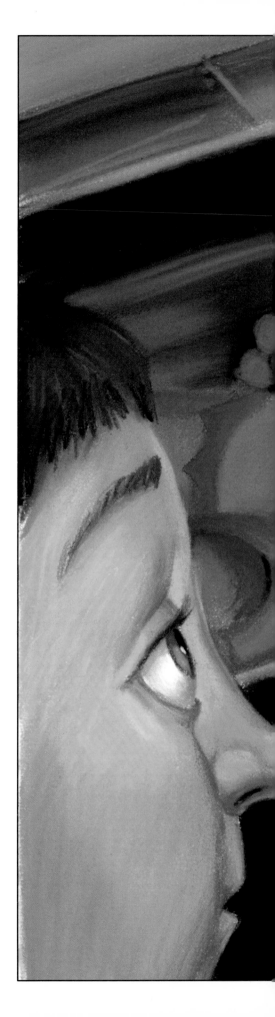

"CARTWHEELS!"

Harvey almost shouted it, and Uncle Kaz jerked back his head in surprise.

"Cartwheels?" he said.

"Last year, in second grade, we had to learn to do cartwheels. I couldn't, at first, but I kept trying and trying. And one day I could. I *like* to do cartwheels."

"Then cartwheels it is!" announced Uncle Kaz. "Or, at least, that will be the main part of your act."

"The main part?" asked Harvey, a little concerned.

"Sure. You can't just do cartwheels. You've got to build an act around that. A little juggling. A little magic, maybe. But don't worry, I can teach you how to do those things. OK?"

Harvey nodded his head a little hesitantly. He wasn't sure about those other things, but he figured he could try. He'd managed cartwheels, hadn't he? He smiled at Uncle Kaz and headed for the door.

"One more thing," Uncle Kaz called, waving the poster. "You'd better come up with a name. A stage name. Something people will notice."

It wasn't until two days later that a special name, a really *noticeable* name actually hit Harvey. Mrs. Finchley, his teacher, was talking about geography. And, as usual, Harvey wasn't paying much attention.

But somewhere between the cattle ranches on the Mexican border and the dairy farms in Wisconsin, he got an idea.

Harvey rushed home and and started to draw furiously. Within an
hour, he had made a poster. He rolled it up, wrapped a rubber band
around it, and knocked on his uncle's door.

"What have you got there, behind your back?" asked Uncle Kaz.

"It's a poster," said Harvey. "A poster that people will notice. With a
name they'll notice, too." He unrolled it and held it in front of him.

The first thing Uncle Kaz did was to cock his head and squint really hard. And after he'd finished squinting, Uncle Kaz grinned. Slowly and proudly, he read: "FROM THE STAGES OF ZANZIBAR, MADRID, AND GAY PAREE—THE ONE AND ONLY DELGADO CHEESE!"

"Delgado Cheese," Uncle Kaz repeated. "It's just the name I would have chosen."

"Really?" said Harvey, lowering the poster so he could see over the top.

"Absolutely! It's…uhhmm…*exotic*, that's what it is."

"Exotic?" asked Harvey, a little worried.

"Yes. Strange but wonderful. Like the cherubim and seraphim. Like manna in the wilderness. Like your Aunt Minnie's spoon collection. And now, Mr. Delgado Cheese, what do you say we start teaching you a few magic tricks?"

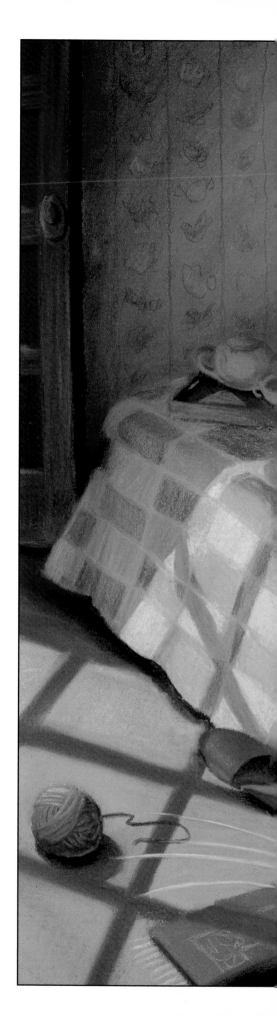

From the stages of Zanzibar, Madrid and Gay Paree...

The One and Only Delgado Cheese!

Over the next few weeks, Harvey—or Delgado Cheese, as he now preferred to be called—stopped by his Uncle Kaz's room after school. For some reason, Uncle Kaz didn't seem to need as much rest as he used to. So Delgado saw him every day.

Using several items hidden away at the bottom of the trunk, Uncle Kaz showed Delgado Cheese a few tricks. He also taught Delgado how to juggle three small oranges.

Then they worked hard to combine the magic and the juggling with the cartwheels, so that Delgado had an "act." Delgado's mother joined in, too, and made him a silky red shirt with flowing sleeves and a pair of bright yellow trousers.

On the day of the talent show, it was plain to everyone in the house that Delgado Cheese was scared. So Uncle Kaz asked him into his room. He had a piece of notepaper and a small envelope lying on his lap desk.

"Who will be introducing the performers tonight?" he asked Delgado.

"My teacher, Mrs. Finchley. Why?"

Uncle Kaz wrote something at the top of the notepaper, folded it, and slid it into the small envelope.

"Give this to Mrs. Finchley tonight," he instructed Delgado.

"All right," said Delgado Cheese. "What is it?"

"It's the *coup de grâce*," smiled Uncle Kaz at a thoroughly puzzled Delgado. "The rainbow after Noah's Flood. The walls of Jericho tumbling down. The final touch to what will be the perfect performance."

Delgado looked solemnly at his feet. "I don't think it's going to be very perfect. I'm really scared."

Uncle Kaz reached over and put one large wrinkled hand on the boy's head. It looked like Delgado was wearing a five-fingered cap. "Your performance will be wonderful. It will have to be. You're doing what you enjoy, right? You're using the talents God gave you, right? And besides, your mother's paid a buck and a half to see the show, and she deserves to get her money's worth."

Delgado looked up. "But what about you? You're coming tonight, aren't you?"

It was Uncle Kaz's turn to look at his feet. "I haven't had any reason to go out of this house for years. And now that I do have a reason, I'm not sure I'm up to it. Maybe I'm like you, Delgado. Maybe I'm just a little scared." He tapped on the note. "You just remember to give this to Mrs. Finchley, like I said."

As he waited behind stage, Delgado Cheese folded and unfolded the small envelope Great Uncle Kaz had given him. He wanted to give it to Mrs. Finchley, but she was busy giving last-minute directions and calming last-minute nerves.

Finally, gulping down his fear and shyness, Delgado pushed his way through the other performers and thrust the note into Mrs. Finchley's hand.

"My uncle asked me to give this to you," he said, as loudly as he dared. "He says it's the *coup de grâce*."

If it had been Harvey Merritt handing her the note, Mrs. Finchley would probably have put it in her pocket without a word. But this little boy didn't exactly look like Harvey Merritt. This little boy didn't speak in that mumbling, unsure way that Harvey Merritt usually spoke. And that's because, as everyone who had a program knew, this little boy was not Harvey Merritt but Delgado Cheese.

Mrs. Finchley opened the envelope and quickly read the note to herself.

She smiled.

"Thank you, Harvey. Excuse me… Thank you, Delgado Cheese," she said.

Delgado Cheese smiled back.

As act followed act, Delgado's fear returned. What did he think he was doing here? What if he goofed? What if he embarrassed himself? He was almost ready to drop his trick cane and his sack of oranges and sneak out, when Mrs. Finchley said, "Delgado Cheese, you're next."

It was too late to run. Too late to go back to being plain old Harvey Merritt.

Mrs. Finchley put her hand on his shoulder. "Just wait one minute," she whispered.

Then she pulled out Great Uncle Kaz's note, stepped up to the microphone and read, in her best ringmaster's voice: "FRESH FROM THE STAGES OF ZANZIBAR, MADRID AND GAY PAREE, EDWARD EVERETT HORTON ELEMENTARY SCHOOL IS PROUD TO PRESENT THAT JUGGLER, ACROBAT AND MAGICIAN EXTRAORDINAIRE— THE ONE, THE ONLY, DELGADO CHEESE!"

The audience applauded. Mrs. Finchley grinned. And Delgado Cheese looked out at the crowd. The lights were so bright that all he could see clearly were the first few rows. But that was all he needed to see. For sitting in his wheelchair at the very front, with his top hat and cane, was Dancin' Dan the Vaudeville Man!

Delgado ran from Mrs. Finchley's side
and cartwheeled onto the stage. Once for
Zanzibar. Twice for Madrid. Three times for
Gay Paree. The audience applauded again.

Delgado Cheese picked up his oranges
and started to toss them in the air. One for
Zanzibar. Two for Madrid. Three for Gay
Paree. He dropped Zanzibar halfway
through, but the people clapped anyway.

Finally Delgado Cheese reached into the
sack and pulled out his magic cane. *Voilà!*
The cane turned into a bunch of flowers. He
called Mrs. Finchley to his side and reached
behind her ear. *Voilà!* There was a fifty-cent
piece. The audience applauded once more.

Delgado Cheese bowed to the audience and smiled. He was using the talents God had given him, and he was enjoying himself. At last he was more than just plain normal. He was being noticed.

But as he stood there amid all the applause, the thing Delgado Cheese noticed most of all was a wrinkled pair of clapping hands in the front row—from Zanzibar, Madrid and Gay Paree.